AF334787

Ruin

Ruin

Patrick Phillips

what books

Library of Congress Cataloging-in-Publication Data
Phillips, Patrick, 1958–
Ruin / Patrick Phillips
        p.   cm.
Contents: Ruin – numbers
ISBN 0-9646535-0-8   (pbk. $8.95)
I. Title

¿ what books

for Laura
&
of my family

Acknowledgements:

I want to thank everyone who has encouraged me during the five years it has taken to write this book, particularly – Kevin Davies and Thad Ziolkowski; Jennifer Moxley, editor of The Impercipient, *for publishing "two"; Thom Gunn for his generous comments on "one"; C.D. Wright for her advice on how* Ruin *and* numbers *talk to each other; and Michael Palmer, Jackson Mac Low, Nancy Shaw, Jeff Hull, Andy Levy, and Peter Gizzi for comments in passing, or in substance, that kept the project going.*

Contents

Ruin

*'This dog is mine,' said those poor children;
'that is my place in the sun' . . .*

Pascal, Pensées #295

Property is theft!

Proudhon, "Qu'est ce que la propriété?"

ball.

as if our folk.

the sun's wrecked face

routs.

out of   the blue

your lips   –   hock.

here.   o is closed

at its sum.

the lack of   rain's a

flat so n so.

someone'skin.

my   last   luring

wall.

the dubious here –

                wool.

    these   clock.

    these   tires.

                worn.

the same   hints a necklace.

       smile – simile.

   an unprovoked wall hits

                  states –

      string of pearls.

surrounded day

            ground

  in its own   ringing

            ground

under touch –

lasts/lassos

–   the coast.

to seldom taste

or rope   of this sleep.

our past.   the air

met with.

and its   total

bearing –

as were us

    how listening

            collapses

sure

    of its own collapsing

              to

  and then

       to

the mid

let-to –

a town.   til

seen.

its   yesterday.

pushed.

before   a later

city –

my sound –

push of even.

day below you.

have.   a   sight.

call

to put to   peek.

or   late

collide

blood.

doubt.

clock of country.

strep.

these two

stare at the skin.

traps.   kissed you.

in some smaller

clothing

no –

single.

a stop to your

rim.

how the last one   stiffs.

stands   clear.

folded

magic.

simple

blinder

am

in a hello of this work

wood   stay

in   the clapping

                of this land

and my

        reside

out.

classed

my   several   houses.

your arm

totters   to

you.   a day –

to - day   –   to - me.

of   late

of   slips . . .

at   most you're

                reigned.

    mere waters

                    flown.

            to the rest.

    skies a   curtain

                sunk

        at the worlds

                    undressing –

your   splayed/sun.

                    scatter

got –   and left

        to its own   water.

in the   street   gun

        of a lingering answer.

                boy.   and

again

        girl.

hurt.

    to my   success.

  more   – day

then cut.

    eye   still with the thing –

     zero.   you

         before-hand

  a story.   or glut

       in our cue.

the wreck   flowers

before   its   close.

        weeks   said

        to your face. lap.

                full to   feel   to

say one last

                        pencil of us.

        late   in the street.

                        – in   brick

before   all   broken

                suns.

my   spill

   my fewer house

chalks.

    a fluke   I.

    round   – in the head.

 given –

    the sprung   tie.

        out of.

tuned   to.

   its   tilted

          go –

the seen   lines.

last   clasp –

a   stray.

the thorough

ton of eye.

a killing.

rapt   hole in the head.

–   took with those.

inside   the flower

and its   rocky

moon

can –

our front door.

lit   week

in its own can.

followed   work.

the hollow

stint

while   broke.

and.

after several days . . .

out-running –

       the line.

  flat or –

        loot.

    level –

  such and such life

       at a pin.

your knife.

   labelled   sky

     in its   blown

scheduling.

I balk

at the sun.

go.

no   work   here.

as if you touch   me.

calamity

– you.

the hole

struck –

before glancing   off.

your   and   my

tattled

body.

booed –

my place   stains.

an open   bulb

stuck with itself.

to see

me

run through your eye.

rote. stem.

one last stare

before the sun   comes on.

and listening to.

and harried

blunder

numbers

where movement, a marker.
there's another, done.
under sky. to
walk a particular rhythm.
fallen – itself murmur,
moisture under its leg. hands
clasped over a box in guessing.

sky, an inheritance.
answer is "parcel of land".
dances, their unbearable questions.

field asks
closet, letter, clutter
(roof of your mouth).

this box is close.
note being passed, there,
along the grass-line.

up close, a string (one which
is heard) recovers. hovers

listing trees overhead.
continue to chest.

rock. what is left of one.
what is to become of one.

acting body.
water on, long, going –
approaching land.

several places listed . . .
ore, dexterity, rid.

some popular responses . . .
basra, song bo, nome.

zero

asking.
the opulent history is
mnemonic here.

this land is your fall.
culminating guesswork.
it settles as now approaches.

zero

clotted, rose and
brick. a family of hours
said across faces and glue –
a direction for they who remember.

zero

> kin, an unquestionable posture.
> gesture for sap, stark.
> chased out midnight.
> swerving oncoming traffic.

zero

> throw. haven't. turn around.
> mesh. cheek. catalogue.

holding your tongue. gifted.
thought as a series of bumps –
(creatures in their element).
to have been told.

zero

reconcilia. house or not.
hearing at cordon. woods.

it's as supposed.
broke in. a trade. plum.
had looked out
and trespassing.
what was to be level.
round in foment.
level and round.
it was a mixture of corners.
story. an answer to calling.
except.

palpable.
the problem as innards.
given to the first person.
glass. hugging.

shape of mis-given.
notice. hush.
clasp, picture in a hurry.
grasping for a fleshy arm.
milk.

let. meet. after noon.

so restless or current.

                      asleep and going to
sleep.
    ahold of apple. a hold at
      wrong ringing
                    or grass

two

blank by you I
     the lapsing verve
my fat body lops
  and the two
bare headed, clear serum
    it to the teeth
                falsetto.
    we've the last clip
      a pattering hole
  herd wistful
     or yesteryear for

that's salt or wax.

flustered at the sun
of there a
mind on a stick.

to pattern, muscle to
have someone standing
by

afterward . . .
e as in see
o as in wearing.

point

     the lap as took, too seen

  cast, ah,

    that post of you

pushed backward, latter,

  mine,

what you will remember

     suffuse

two

help me, I'm.
       cudgel of snow, or
       maybe sun. I
think the world of you.
       curl, peril, hay –
   your harm again,
in/no arm, mine, across.
  afizz.

two

kept
                the scopic hand
            that I live

    the sack of you
                    see to. a were.

    or an adjective hole
            that I   falls

two

done. secret to hill.
                crescent.

   absent that full,
there is a lot to you.
  hole. douse.
         your
            lightening.
outed or almost let.

that we   that trucked

        onus

         a lake bed

         a bed bed wrung

the floated and stung sun

            cup   glued to itself

    hardly   the hand

that the hold what

     I burn

or burned ease

  lateral thickening

    letter of me   turbulent

       perimetric

    coughing orhaving

as though third   and caught

  lasting

     sick at you

white and

    to the world with

three

    lade and

            place

    through the collapse of such

what abrupt world

    fluency skips to its ever

        last among though

          limiting to had

      held

three

things, or strained

                    it to working

        the upper hand,   sight

                    a fit for it

        going to be

an area around a load

how weighted before

crowd

      though cut

           no blown from

the lip tucked under

           or possibly floes

more handed   more level

        by proxy

      what we saw

             less living

if a face –

        told around it

                dapped

    pile of

        foliate   –   exfoliate

    the bit about braille

        sticks

                a night of them

        pun

where the land

        strung and result

        or stem

     underage placed

at the outset

        to we too

not lit, or on

three

as tune to

           dire of it

near that taken world

    palp

        the slight root

ciliate and mistaken

   as go go as

       clung

such sake

    stream to

        corners of all sorts

        history in eddied

          kiss

  flat to touch

the world to the hand

        not the world

play

gotten and the running.

though missed

hasp and　　　　lift.

a slackening

careen look.

would up.

wooded.

could lie to.

always lied.

and parade –

put to –

       part

              cut

           he, she,

            city

claimed or claim

             so to

stood

         stood

one

land and turned

ness

the opened   half facing world

the other   rock

glass   –   in   ran

toward it/no to   your

that complete   round

the ruin to be left

hazard

foil

seen out

have been

or yo-yo

I too see I   too country

    delapidate   a spoken

        flow town

        one or two   people

the count and conjugal   that

           to the waist

      and above   this

      city

one

were range

        sure.

the letting in –

      its circular thing.

  clear   –   derange.

      so much for it

the plain and half

        implement.

to loose   again

one

on

            until or reserve

            palate.

its hill and walkway   run –

        string   end,

                the curved

            remedy   a thought

                a plastic.

                    tool

        call   and into

            place

one

                        some

         and in   position

                 orbit

                          window

         gloss   –   this train

                    piece of work

    that verge

                      hole melody

         the wrung

                   its mile of me

how color

       or plan.

  such ability   my breach

       -ment.   our

     fluent aloft seen.

       the plain torn

  sun.

      and more for you

perhaps   sky –

                 its glue.

   while   a move

        termed   where

                   living is   off

                          a land

      or query   as were

            as the too

of several minds

                   and many

one

law or

    scape.

        its view

    the half sky's   done

            – a litter.

  to repeat   the hand

     the hand   is

under.   as run to

  its often

     ground

one

the face

        among its shape

    curl – and

work of   say   carried

      place

the city   it does go

      see the line

            moves

      in lieu of its own

calendar

      goes

how   to have

                when

                        the look   a furl

                                today

        lore   and you   is fit

        its lake –

                        had is halving

                and its partner

one

the took and   music

            cumulate

                  the different lobe

      and hand   in answer

      our movement   a work

            or   stands

                  on this spot

Cover Photo:

Near the "old 61 hi-way" in Osceola, Arkansas (between St. Louis and Memphis), there was an old blues house called the Dispsy Doodle where a host of Delta blues giants once played. On a search for the place, my father and brothers and I saw an enormous cloud of smoke and followed it to find the fire department (that day all white men) setting fire to a house on the "black side of town." After asking around, it turned out the Dipsy Doodle had burned down years earlier and that this house had tried in one way or another to take its place as a juke joint and music hall. According to neighbors, the city had tried to shut it down several times – as it had become a "nuisance." Since people continued to use the place, the fire department burned the house to the ground.

I took this photo to document the event and as a reminder to myself that the poet's house is always on fire.

note on ¿ what books:

they began to exist–error
if error vertigo their sun
eyes delirium–both initial together
rove into the blue initial
surely it carves a breath

Zukofsky, "A" 22